6TH GRADE REVENGERS
2

THE
SUBSTITUTE CRIMINAL

STEVEN WHIBLEY

Published by Steven Whibley Publishing
Victoria, British Columbia
www.stevenwhibley.com

Editing: Maya Packard
Copyediting: Chandler Groover
Cover Design: Pintado (rogerdespi.8229@gmail.com)
Interior Layout and Design: Tammy Desnoyers (www.tammydesign.ca)

Library and Archives Canada Cataloguing in Publication

Whibley, Steven, 1978-, author
       The substitute criminal / Steven Whibley.

(6th grade revengers ; 2)
Issued in print and electronic formats.
ISBN 978-1-927905-10-4 (paperback).--ISBN 978-1-927905-09-8 (pdf)

       I. Title.

PS8645.H46S83 2015   jC813'.6   C2015-905595-4
                                               C2015-905596-2

For Isaiah and Aubree

– Steven Whibley

CHAPTER 1

The gun felt slick in my hands. Cold. But a comfortable cold. It belonged in my hands. I peeked around the corner to look for my target. No sign of him. A can rattled behind the concrete pillar to my right. I stepped out. The hairs on the back of my neck tingled. Something wasn't right. I turned and spotted movement. A shadow. Marcus darted out from a shelter behind me. I raised the end of my gun and shot first. Marcus fell to the ground in a dramatic death.

Then he looked up. "I still nailed you three to two."

I shot him again. Paint exploded over his chest in another splat of blue.

He raised his gun and fired two shots that exploded against my chest. I was about to return fire again when he raised his hands. "Okay, okay, enough. Truce!"

I nodded and lowered my gun and smiled. "You're supposed to yell HIT when you get hit, remember?"

He crawled back to his feet and rubbed the spot where I'd hit him. "Ow! Next time I'm wearing three sweaters under this." He tugged at his dark coveralls with the PAINT DEATH logo on the shoulder. "But you saw me get hit," he said, poking me in the chest. "And you know it's against the rules to shoot a man while he's down."

I shrugged. "Revengers play by their own rules."

He laughed and put his arms out to the side. "You really think this helps us? I mean, we're Revengers, not assassins. We're not killers." He pulled off his goggles and wiped the sweat out of his eyes.

"We need all the skills we can get—and that includes sharpening our stalking skills." I glanced up at the sky. "We should get back."

I figured we had about an hour left of sunlight. We'd started coming to the paintball park after school every Tuesday and Thursday. I'd told Marcus we needed killer instincts if we were going to stay in the Revenger business. But he was right. We didn't really kill people. We made problems disappear. Sometimes those problems were people. Other times, like our first job, those problems were animals. Specifically, a beast we called Evil Cat who terrorized a nearby neighborhood. We trapped the cat, took him to the vet for treatment, and safely delivered him back home to his thankful owner. The neighborhood's problem did disappear, but in the end it felt more like a good deed than true Revenger business.

"It's working," I told him, as we stripped out of our protective gear. "We're sharper."

"Whatever you say." Marcus groaned and then said, "Dude, my mom is going to kill me if I come home with blue all over this shirt. It's new."

The coveralls stopped most of the paint, but if you got shot around the neck or right on the zipper the way Marcus had, the paint got through. He had blue marks on his shirt.

"It'll wash out. And your mom won't even notice. But you can come home with me and wash it there if you're worried."

"Nah, I should be okay."

That was obvious. Marcus's parents were pretty cool about whatever Marcus was into. Only-child syndrome, he called it. When you're the only child the attention is all on you so you get more attention than kids from bigger families—at least that's what Marcus said. I had two sisters so maybe my parents split their attention between us, but then I had two more people watching my every move. I was pretty sure I had more attention, not less.

I followed Marcus out of the park. "Listen, I'm not kidding. I really think coming here and practicing this stuff is helping us. It's sharpening our senses." I waved at the park. "I could feel you sneaking up on me."

Marcus snorted. He stuffed his hands in his jeans pockets. He'd been my best friend since forever. He was also my partner-in-not-so-much-crime and the mastermind behind our website.

"We need another really good request to come in," I said. "Something to push our business over the next hump. We're not getting the kind of requests I want us to get. Nothing super challenging. I'm worried we're going to get rusty."

"That reminds me," Marcus said. "I gotta go home and check the email. We can't afford to crash the server again or my dad's going to start asking questions about how much traffic we're getting. Besides, it hasn't been that long since we had a good target walk into our sights. What about Duce?"

I smiled. We'd taken on a few nothing jobs since we launched our business. A couple bullies in neighboring schools were no longer bothering their classmates. Duce—the guy Marcus was talking about—was one job I had been happy to take on. He was the kind of bully you read about in the newspapers. He beat up kids, stole from them, scared them, made life in the halls a living nightmare for that school. We actually received more than one request for help dealing with this one guy.

It was a pretty good job, but as good as it felt to get rid of him, it really had been too easy. It took us all of three days to come up with a plan for the bully and an afternoon to implement it.

His name wasn't really Duce, that's just what we called him on account of the kind of Revengering we dished out. We started by writing his name on the elastic band of a bunch of tighty-whitey underwear—big capital letters in felt pen. Full name, even his middle name so there was no mistaking who the underwear belonged to. Then we strategically put melted chocolate on them so it looked like the guy, well, *duced* his pants... all the time. Then we left them all over the school. We taped them to his locker, hung them from the basketball nets, scattered them in high-traffic areas of the school, and even put a couple pairs on the desks of teachers whose classes he had.

It was effective. Ruthless, by some standards, but not the challenge I was looking for.

"We have an awesome site," Marcus said. "We're building a reputation. As long as we keep our eyes and ears open, that next big job will come along. It'll probably just step right into our path. It'll be so obvious we won't be able to avoid it if we try."

Turned out Marcus was totally right. The following day we—the Revengers—were given the opportunity of a lifetime.

CHAPTER 2

I'd stayed up all night working on my history assignment. I was exhausted but confident. And when the classroom door opened I expected to see Ms. Blindly. Ms. Blindly was a total rock star, one of those teachers who really understands her students.

There wasn't a kid in the entire school who didn't love her. One of the reasons I'd done my homework was because I didn't want to disappoint her.

But when I saw the man who walked into the class—the man we all knew too well—I joined with the rest of my class as we released a collective groan.

Mr. Shevchenko smiled when he heard it. It was such an awkward name we all called him "Mr. Shev" but not to his face. That he fed off the misery of his students was only one of the many rumors about this substitute teacher. Some of the others had him hanging around retirement homes at night and mugging the elderly. Or that he was one of America's most wanted criminals and had been hiding out as a lowly middle school sub for the last few years, biding his time before he went on another crime spree. My personal favorite was that instead of milk on his morning cereal, he used the tears of orphans. Honestly, all of those could have been true. It might also have been true, however, that he was just a jerk who loved giving out detentions.

"Good morning, class." Mr. Shev's accent always reminded me of someone trying to fake it as a vampire from an old movie. It made my skin crawl. Going by the shivers of everyone around me, I wasn't the only one. "As you may have guessed, Ms. Blindly will not be here today, or—" He licked his lips, pausing for a moment before finishing his sentence, "—for the rest of the week."

Marcus dropped his head onto his desk, and a second groan rose up around me.

"There is even a possibility," he added, "she will be gone for the rest of the semester."

From her front row, center seat, Janet Everton, who had to know everything about everyone, asked, "Is she sick? I hadn't heard anything like that. Was she in an accident? Is she okay?"

Mr. Shev stepped so close to her desk she had to crane her neck back to see his face.

He cleared his throat. "Ms....?"

"Everton. Janet Everton."

Shevchenko nodded. "Well, Ms. Everton, you have earned yourself two afternoons of detention."

It was as if Mr. Shev had just said something to Janet in Japanese, or Swahili, or some other foreign language. She blinked at him. "Pardon me?"

"Detention, Ms. Everton. You will report here at the end of school today, and tomorrow as well."

She shook her head. "I don't understand."

"Well, then three days ought to give you plenty of time to figure it out. You've earned another day for yourself. Congratulations."

Realization settled on Janet. Her shoulders slumped like a deflating balloon. "You mean just because I asked if Ms. Blindly was okay?"

"Because you spoke without first raising your hand." He pointed at her. "Which you have done yet again, and so you are now up to four days of detention. Speak again and you'll have the full week."

Janet didn't get in trouble... ever. Not by Ms. Blindly. Not by any other substitute teacher we'd ever had. In fact, in the dozen or so times we'd had Mr. Shevchenko I couldn't remember him punishing her. Which was probably why he didn't know her name.

From the back of the room I could see her ears redden. It must've taken all her effort but she kept her mouth shut. Janet wouldn't cry. She'd go out at recess and stomp around, shout about it, maybe even kick a tree or something, but she didn't go in for tears.

"I think I have a candidate for our next target," Marcus whispered to me.

"Marcus Yardley," Mr. Shev called from the front of the room. "I know your name. Thank you for speaking out of turn. You and your partner in crime will get to join Ms. Everton for the first day of her detention."

"Partner in crime?" Marcus asked.

Putting up my hand and waving it, I told him, "I didn't say a word."

Shevchenko clapped his hands together and rubbed them. "This is marvelous. The two of you just earned four days in detention. At least Ms. Everton won't be lonely." He cast his gaze around the room. "Anyone else want to join them?"

Marcus glanced at me with his mouth hanging open. I shook my head and mouthed, "Don't speak." Turning to the front of the room, Mr. Shev glared at me.

"Something you want to add, Mr. Moter?"

I shook my head. I didn't say a word. But what I wanted to say was, "Alex Shevchenko, prepare to meet the Revengers."

CHAPTER 3

By lunch seven of us had been scheduled for detention and by the end of the day that had risen to twelve. When the last bell rang only a little over half the class left. Those who did ran for the exit as if zombies had just come in through the windows. Mr. Shev sat on the edge of Ms. Blindly's desk and shook his head at the twelve who remained. "I'm disappointed in all of you. I know it's common practice to give the substitute teacher a hard time, but I thought we," he gestured to himself and then to the rest of us in a sweeping motion that reminded me of a ringmaster, "were different. I thought you saw me as something more than just a substitute." He tsked and added, "I think maybe you've all just forgotten how much history we've had together." He clapped his hands and stood. "Pull out a pen and paper. You can leave detention as soon as you write out your first memory of me. When do you recall first having me as a teacher? I think writing it out would be helpful in reminding yourself that I've been part of your educational experience for quite some time. You will each read your work aloud before you leave."

Everyone started muttering to each other and more than

one person said, "What is he talking about?"

He snapped his fingers and cast a glare around the room. I pulled out a sheet of paper.

The first memory I had of Mr. Shevchenko came from first grade. He'd been a substitute for Mrs. Meister. During lunch—which we ate at our desks—I remembered him wandering the room, plucking items from our lunch bags and eating them. I had a piece of strawberry fruit leather I'd been saving until the end of my lunch. It was my favorite back then—still is—and he walked up and took it off my desk as if stealing food was totally allowed. He didn't even try to hide what he'd done.

I wanted to write that out. I wanted him to know that he wasn't at all respected and that pretty much everyone hated him. But I needed to be smart. I needed to think like a Revenger. If I was going to take the man out of commission, I needed to stay off his radar.

The only problem was, I didn't have a plan yet—except to avoid more detention.

In the end I wrote about how he'd helped direct a Christmas concert during second grade. He'd talked about how he nearly became a famous stage actor, but decided to be a substitute instead. Even at seven years old I knew how ridiculous that was. Worse than his bragging was the way he'd talked to the cast as if we were not very good Broadway veterans. He told one kid he looked constipated when he sang, and another that her voice had the squeaking quality of a caffeine-addicted chimpanzee—whatever that meant. Both kids went home crying more than once, but Mr. Shev didn't notice or didn't care.

Still, I left those things out of my paper and kept the focus on his fantasy of his own brilliance.

"Ah yes," he said when I'd finished reading my paragraph to the class. "I played Othello in college, you know. I'd only been in the country for a couple years—having arrived from Ukraine as I might have mentioned."

He had mentioned it. Multiple times.

"My English wasn't perfect at the time," he continued.

"Still isn't," Marcus whispered.

I coughed to cover up my laugh and Shev glared at me before continuing. "I even had a bit of an accent. Probably hard to believe hearing me talk now. But I landed the lead in a Shakespeare play. I had a promising career ahead of myself. But alas..." Standing, he looked up at the ceiling. "I felt a calling to work with children and mold youth into our future leaders."

"And we're so grateful." I had to consciously stop myself from rolling my eyes.

"Any chance you'll be heading back to the Ukraine to visit anytime soon?" Marcus asked.

Shev's eyes narrowed. "I haven't seen my family in years, but I hope I'll be able to go there soon. I'd love to reconnect with them."

He seemed almost sad about it, but Shev was heartless, and I was pretty sure you needed a heart to be sad.

He called on the next student and one by one everyone else shared uninteresting stories of Shevchenko subbing for various subjects and teachers. Most were half-true and watered down so Mr. Shev didn't get angry. Marissa Lewis talked about how in the fourth grade she was impressed with how Mr. Shev had kept control of some of the kids by making them write sentences over and over. But I remembered that day. I'd been one of the kids writing sentences. What Marissa had left out was the fact that our sentences had to say, "I will not speak out in Mr. Shevchenko's class because he is the greatest teacher on the planet and we love him." It had been infuriating.

I glared at him. I was going to be smart about this. I'd stay off his radar. But payback was coming, Mr. Shev.

Turning to Marcus, Shevchenko said, "And finally, Mr. Yardly, would you please share what you remember about our first meeting?"

Marcus cleared his throat. I knew that what he was about to say wouldn't be helpful to our mission. I tried to give him various eye signals to warn him, but he didn't see me. I was pretty sure I looked like I was having a massive face spasm.

"In third grade," Marcus began, "you were the substitute for Mrs. Tan's class the week after Halloween."

Mr. Shev nodded as if he remembered the time well. But I knew where this was going and it was nowhere good. I cleared my throat, shifted in my seat, stretched my arms above my head—anything to grab Marcus's attention. Nothing worked. I didn't even attract Mr. Shev's attention; he was so caught up in his own memories.

"I remember," Marcus continued, "because I had brought two mini chocolate bars from my trick-or-treating. I was saving them for after lunch, but before I could even take the first bite of my PB&J, you came by and snatched the chocolate from my desk and ate it. Right in front of everyone." He looked up and eyed Shevchenko, who had stopped nodding and stared at my friend with narrowed eyes and a clenched jaw.

"I think you have me mistaken for another teacher," Shevchenko said.

"No, it was you. But don't worry, I don't look at it like you stole from me. I look at it like you saved me from getting a cavity." Marcus smiled. "So thank you so much."

No one in the room moved a muscle. I'm pretty sure we all couldn't believe what we were seeing. Marcus held his ground, smiling at Shevchenko like he was a sweet old man. Shevchenko, on the other hand, looked like he was about to explode.

Slowly, and some would say bravely, Janet raised her hand.

"Yes?" Shevchenko asked, without looking away from Marcus. "What is it, Ms. Everton?"

"Well, um, I was just wondering." She wet her lips and coughed, and it was clear that even someone as brave as Janet felt a little intimidated by Mr. Shev. "What I mean is, I think I speak for everyone when I say we're really happy you're here." Shevchenko turned to Janet with a raised eyebrow. She plowed forward like a soldier heading into battle without a gun. "I think we're all curious about the health of Ms. Blindly. Is she in the hospital? Or out of town? How is it possible she'll be gone all semester?"

It had to be driving Janet bat-crazy not knowing what was going on with Ms. Blindly. Mr. Shev knew it as well, or seemed to. But I had a feeling he was underestimating the resources Janet had at her disposal. If he didn't tell her, she'd find out another way. Janet knew people all over town and she wasn't afraid to talk to them. She regularly babysat for Ms. Abrahams, the school office secretary. Janet's mom worked at the most popular hair salon in town, which practically every woman in town visited at some point. Janet often helped out there, and from what I heard from my mom, the gossip was as easy to get as sand at the beach.

Still, Mr. Shev seemed determined to keep Janet in the dark as long as possible. Probably just because he was mean like that. "I'm not at liberty to pass it along to a bunch of children. Just know that you and your classmates will be in my capable hands."

He nodded at the clock. "You've all been here long enough today." He seemed to be telling us to go, and Marcus and Andrew Levi stood to go. He raised an eyebrow and smiled at Marcus. "I didn't dismiss you yet. You two have another day's detention. That's the whole week for you, Mr. Yardly. Congratulations."

Marcus smiled and bowed before plopping back in his chair.

"You're all dismissed," Shevchenko said.

Storm clouds rolled overhead as we walked home. Sky went home with one of her friends from school so we didn't have to walk her. Grayness seemed to permeate the street and the cookie-cutter homes we passed along the way. But my mood probably had something to do with that. Marcus spoke when we were a few blocks from the school. "Tell me you have a plan. That guy is an even bigger jerk than I remembered."

I shook my head. "I don't have a plan yet, but it's forming. I can feel it. I need more time. What about you? Any ideas?

"Several. I say we slowly make him go insane—or at least make him think he's gone insane. We could create some sort of water leak right over his desk—slow dripping, all day long. Oh! Or we could make him think he's gone deaf. You know, we could all pretend to be talking but not really make a sound. If we play our cards right he might end up in the super crazy ward in the hospital. In one of those little padded rooms in a straitjacket." He laughed. "I'd pay money to see that."

"Yeah," I said, thinking over his ideas. They were crazy, all right. "But if we can pull off getting rid of a teacher, our Revenger reputation would be concrete. Imagine all the kids willing to throw their allowances at us to take their teachers out of commission for a few days."

"If we're going to pull that off, we better have a killer plan for how to get rid of Shev. Something that drops people's jaws when they hear about it. Plus, it'll have to be totally clear that we were responsible."

"The Revengers," I said. "Not us specifically—the Revengers need to get the credit."

"That's what I meant," Marcus said. He snapped his fingers. "Oh, what about this?" He turned to face me, walking backwards. "Hide his keys in his shoes. Or put dog turds in the pockets of his jacket? Break into his house and put double of everything he has in his fridge so he thinks he bought everything twice. I mean, that would totally make a guy go crazy."

"Not a bad idea, but it's not big enough. Besides, I don't think we want to break and enter this early on."

"We need to be ruthless," Marcus said. "I'm sick of people emailing the Revengers asking us to turn them into rock stars."

I groaned at that. My sister's jerk boyfriend had been one

of our first targets as Revengers. He was a loser who treated me and my sister like garbage. We manipulated an online video of him singing on the street and made it look like he had thousands of fans. Then we tricked him into leaving the city, to no longer bother me and Ronie. It all worked like we'd planned, except that he ended up landing a recording contract and was now climbing the charts.

"You're right. We'll hit Shev with everything we've got. Show the world what the Revengers are really made of. He's the perfect target too, since he thinks he can treat us any way he wants and there's nothing we can do about it." I clenched my fists. "I mean, he ate your candy! What grown person eats a kid's candy?"

"A crazy one," Marcus agreed.

"Okay, here's what I think. We need it to be very clear that the Revengers are taking Shev down. So I say we private message the whole class—everyone including ourselves—and say that The Revengers have been commissioned to take out Mr. Shev. Make sure that tip button is extra big so they can donate when we succeed."

"There might be a few who rat us out, you know."

I shook my head. "They'll rat out the Revengers. I don't care about that. I don't care if Shev knows he's a marked guy. As long as they can't trace it back to us, we're gold."

Marcus nodded excitedly. "Awesome. I can't wait. So, can I assume you have a plan brewing in that head of yours?"

"Yeah, I have something brewing."

"Well, what is it? Are you going to somehow get the guy fired?"

"Nah," I said, starting to smile. "Something even better."

CHAPTER 4

I totally spaced out during dinner, I was thinking so much about taking down Mr. Shev. Mom had to ask me three times if I wanted to play soccer later in the year. The third time Mom asked, my big sister Ronie kicked me under the table to get my attention. I yelled at her, which made Dad yell at me.

After dinner I shut myself in my room to do homework but I ended up just searching the net for ways to make someone go crazy. I wasn't too excited about trying to get my hands on any of the illegal drugs several of the articles mentioned. And while a massive head injury would probably work, it really wasn't the direction I wanted to take the Revengers. I wanted to be smart about it. Original. So head injuries or anything that could land me in jail for a long time were totally out.

After a few minutes I got an email from our account: TheRevengers@Revengers.com.

Dear student of Mr. Shevchenko's sixth grade class. I hereby accept your proposal to remove your teacher—Mr. Shevchenko—from his position. Payments can be made in the form of a tip on the website. I never fail. Everything that happens from this point on is part of the plan. One way or another, Shevchenko's days are numbered.

The email made me smile. If we pulled this off, word-of-mouth about our business would take off, and we'd start making some real money. I knew we could make Mr. Shev disappear from our school and our lives—forever.

I turned my attention back to my original search for how to make someone crazy and stumbled on something that kicked my creative side into gear. As a plan formed, my smile widened.

Diarrhea-inducing gummy bears.

The reviews had me laughing so hard I was sure my stomach muscles would be sore tomorrow.

Some people called them "the gummy bear cleanse" while others referred to them as "Devil candies." My favorite review came from a construction worker who said he had three of the candies before climbing onto a roof to do some work and within minutes he had to decide if he should leap off the building to get to the outhouse or just squat over the edge.

The best part was that they weren't designed to cause diarrhea. They weren't joke candies. They just used a sugar substitute that virtually every single person who ate them couldn't tolerate. If something happened and Mr. Shev figured out where they'd come from, or that they were the cause of his permanent seat on the toilet, we could play dumb.

It wasn't going to get him out of our lives, but it was a decent phase one. The best part was that it was going to be so easy to get him to eat them.

Easier than giving candy to a baby.

"Gummy bears?" Marcus said when I called him that night. "That's what you think of when you think of Revengers? It's too juvenile. If we're going to decommission this guy we need to be smarter, more original."

"Decommission him?" I asked.

"I'm trying out some new terminology. You know, so we sound more legit. You don't think it worked?"

"No, I don't. And did you even *read* the reviews on the website I sent you? The gummy bear idea is brilliant! Remember, it's just the first phase of the plan."

"Brilliantly childish. Why don't we rig something on his chair that electrocutes him when he sits down?"

"How many times do I have to tell you—we don't actually want to kill him. Creating an electric chair for a teacher would make us crazier than him. But *decommissioning* a teacher who is known for stealing candy from kids by giving him gummy bears like the ones I found online is perfect."

I knew by Marcus's silence he liked my using his "decommissioning" term—even if it was the first and last time he'd hear me use it.

"If it doesn't work," he said finally, "can we at least entertain the idea of putting him through some electro-shock treatments? I read that that kind of stuff actually made people go insane back in the day." I could practically hear his smile. "Wouldn't that be awesome?"

"Um, no. It wouldn't be awesome, and you're starting to scare me with all your talk of electrocuting him. Besides, what if he did become insane and didn't get fired? Then we'd have created another monster, only this one wouldn't be singing— well, maybe he would, but I don't like the idea of a genuinely insane Shevchenko."

Marcus seemed to think about that. "Fair point. I just really wanted to *get* this guy, you know? Pull out all the stops. Go full-on DEFCON 5 on him."

I laughed. "DEFCON 5 is actually not that bad. DEFCON 1 is bad, DEFCON 5 means no danger."

"You know what I mean." I could hear him pacing in his room, something he did when his brain really started working.

"Okay, what do we need to do?"

"Nothing. There's a health food shop downtown that sells them. I already called and put some on hold. I'll pick them up in the morning so let's just meet at school instead of walking in together."

"They're already on hold? So you decided about this before talking to me?"

"I figured if we didn't use them on him, I'd give them to you for your next birthday."

"Oh, thanks. You really think this is going to help with the overall plan?"

"I think it'll get rid of him for a day—and that's a start. The next day we do something else, and the day after that too. It might take a week but eventually he'll get the idea that staying in our class is hazardous to his health."

CHAPTER 5

My little sister Sky and I stopped at the health store on our way to school the next morning. I kept telling her it was a candy store and she had to swear not to tell anyone we'd gone there.

"You don't want us to get in trouble for getting candy, do you?" I asked her.

With wide eyes, she shook her head.

"Good," I told her, and promised I'd buy her something.

When I told the clerk what I was there for, he started laughing. "Whoever you're giving these to better deserve it."

I paid for the gummies and bought Sky a ginger lollipop— the closest thing to candy they had, aside from the gummy bears. She took one lick, made a face, and threw it in the next trash can.

I walked Sky to her classroom, doubled back outside, and met Marcus in the park behind the school. He handed me a clear plastic baggie we'd use to make the treat look like something from a lunch bag.

"So that's it?" Marcus asked after we'd filled the baggie. "We just leave them on Ms. Blindly's desk?"

"If we know Mr. Shev, he'll spot them right away. I bet he eats the whole bag before lunch. It's simple, I know, but it's going to be effective."

Marcus shook his head and let out a breath. "I just don't think we're going to make a large enough hit on him with this."

"For the last time, Marcus, this is phase one. He'll know someone did something to him. He won't know what. If someone told him about our email he'll assume the Revengers got to him. He'll freak out. Tomorrow we'll do something bigger."

"Like an electric chair?" Marcus asked hopefully.

I shook my head and stared at him. "Give it up."

We went into school as if we'd never broken a rule in our lives. There weren't many people in the room yet and those who were there were getting things ready or chatting or playing with their cell phones. I walked to the front of the room, pretended to examine a map on the wall, and dropped the baggie onto the desk. Marcus stood behind me, shielding me. When we turned, no one seemed to have seen anything — or if they had, it hadn't registered as a red flag. I was pretty sure no one noticed.

We took our seats at the back of the room like perfect angels and waited for Mr. Shev to arrive.

With each passing minute, Marcus shifted in his seat, becoming more and more excited. He leaned over to me. "What if he starts eating them right away? Before class starts I mean."

I shrugged. "Let him. The sooner he eats them, the sooner

he'll be stuck on a toilet."

"How long does it take to kick in?" Marcus asked.

"A couple of the reviews said they bought them for their kids and they worked within minutes, but for some people it seemed to take longer."

"Taken out by gummy-bear induced explosive diarrhea," Marcus said with a smile. "At least no one will say the Revengers aren't original."

It seemed the entire class didn't want to give Mr. Shev a reason to hand out more detentions because no one was late. And Shevchenko's usual eagle eye didn't spot the bag of treats in the first five seconds of class, which surprised me.

"Maybe he's going blind," Marcus whispered. "Or he lost his edge and is becoming a nicer person."

"Marcus Yardly!" Shevchenko called from the front of the class. "I see yesterday's detention taught you nothing. You've just earned all of next week as well."

"Guess not," Marcus muttered.

"What was that?" Mr. Shev asked.

"Oh, sorry, I was just saying I deserved that," Marcus answered, smiling. "I shouldn't have been talking. I interrupted and I promise it won't happen again as long as I live..." His smile widened. "As long as *you* live."

It might not have been so bad if Marcus had ended it there, but he didn't. As soon as he finished his last word he started to laugh, and not a normal good-natured chuckle but a full-on creepy laugh. Like one of those evil geniuses on TV who laugh just before they pull a lever on a trap door into a pit filled with hungry lions.

I tried to give him my best "Are you crazy? Shut-up!" look, which he must've understood because he pulled himself together, pressed his lips tight, and slouched in his chair.

"Oh-kay," Shevchenko said, licking his lips. "That was... different. But thank you, Marcus. I look forward to discussing it with you further over the next *several* days." His gaze caught the corner of the bag. He turned and finally took in the bag of treats sitting in the middle of his desk.

I could practically see the glint in his eyes. Shevchenko folded his hands behind his back, walked slowly over, and picked up the candy. He opened the bag. Pulling out a gummy bear, he tossed it into his mouth before reaching back inside the bag.

"I think those are for Ms. Blindly," Marcus said.

"Wow," Mr. Shevchenko said. "You must love detention. Another day for you. But just to be clear, why would you think these are for Ms. Blindly when she's not here and these weren't here yesterday?"

"Because no one would give you a treat," Daniel Davis muttered too loudly from the back of the room.

Most of the class sniggered. I even heard a muttered, "Burn!" A second later the room became quiet as a crypt when Shevchenko swung his arm and one of the gummy bears flew out of his hand and sailed across the room toward Daniel. I don't think Mr. Shev meant to throw it. I think he meant to point at Daniel and forgot he had one in his hands. But I think everyone else thought he'd thrown it.

It was just a gummy bear and it's not like it would hurt to get hit by it, but Daniel's instinct was to duck. He quickly lowered his head—too hard and fast. His face smashed into the edge of his desk. The *thwap* echoed across the room. When he raised his head, blood dripped from his nose.

Daniel moaned and held his face. The blood seeped through his fingers. Everyone around him cringed back. Shevchenko turned white. He quickly walked over to Daniel, pulled him up, and escorted him out of the room. As he left he shouted behind him, "Open your history books to chapter three and do the questions at the end of the chapter." As soon as the door shut behind them, the class erupted. Nobody could believe what had just happened.

Marcus turned toward me. "I think Shevchenko looks like a forty-two regular."

"What are you talking about?"

"Just sizing him up for his straitjacket. Dude's crazy already."

Shevchenko wasn't gone five minutes before he came back... alone. His face was scrunched up tight, and I wondered how he had explained Daniel's injury to the school nurse. Maybe he'd get fired and we wouldn't have to worry about the gummy bears.

No one spoke while Mr. Shev made his way to the front of the class. He pulled out the chair from behind the desk and dropped into it hard. A moment later, from all the way across the room I heard Shevchenko's stomach gurgle.

"Mr. Paulson," Shevchenko said as he stood up.

Bryce Paulson was the suck-up of the class. Short and scrawny, he was always desperate for attention and approval from anyone—teachers mostly. But even he kept a low profile around Mr. Shev.

"Yes, s-sir?" Bryce said, stuttering.

"Take a seat at my desk. I have to step out for a few moments to... er, check on Daniel. If anyone gives you trouble or does anything short of sitting and reading the assigned chapter and doing the questions, you are to write their names down for detention."

Bryce scampered to the desk and plopped himself into the

chair, looking more scared than proud to be teacher's pet.

Marcus leaned back in his chair and smiled. It took all my effort not to do the exact same thing.

The bag of gummy bears sat on the edge of the desk. Shevchenko grabbed another one and threw it into his mouth, almost defiantly, like he wanted to show us that he was still winning.

Bryce eyed the candy like a wolf eying a fat rabbit.

"Since you are assuming my position, Mr. Paulson," Shevchenko said, "you may have one. But only one." He glanced over his shoulder and sneered at the rest of us, trying to look tough and in control but honestly, his face had gone a little green. "Perhaps if you're on good behavior while I'm gone, Mr. Paulson can give one or two of you one of these as a reward."

I did laugh at that, not only because the reward for good behavior would be explosive diarrhea, but because Shevchenko actually thought gummy bears would be a good reason for good behavior. I mean, give me a break. I loved candy as much as the next guy, but not getting some wasn't going to reduce me to tears. I'd stopped getting that emotional about candy when I'd turned six.

Bryce made a scene of licking his lips and putting his hand over the gummies in the bag, hovering, as if he was having a tough choice between the flavors.

"One," Shevchenko said again.

Bryce plucked one from the bag and made a show of

tossing it in his mouth.

"Enjoy it," Marcus whispered. "You deserve it."

Shevchenko buckled at the waist suddenly and clutched his stomach. "I'll be back." He trotted to the door as if trying to hold something in.

Which, of course, made me and Marcus do a quick fist bump.

Mr. Shev wasn't out of the class one second before Bryce offered the gummy bears to his eager friends, who each had at least two.

I'd never seen something take effect so quickly. It was only a few minutes after Bryce had eaten his gummy that he suddenly jumped up from behind the desk and clenched his backside with his hands. "Oh no, oh no, oh no," he whimpered as he sprinted for the door. He hit it without slowing down.

The closest toilet was at least a hundred yards away. He wasn't going to make it. A couple people laughed at his quick departure and someone said, "Maybe he needs a diaper." But a few second later Bryce's friends rushed out of the room in the same way. They were going to destroy that bathroom.

"Four for the price of one," Marcus said.

While they were gone, a couple others snuck up to the desk to have a gummy bear. I wanted to warn everyone, but if I did that someone would put it together and I'd be in trouble. As much as I hated seeing innocent victims walk up there and chomp down a gummy bear, it wasn't as if it was going to cause any real lasting damage—okay, there might be some ruined pairs of underwear, but that was about it.

Five minutes seemed to be magic time. I timed a few of the people who ate the gummies and it was almost right on the five-minute mark. Within fifteen minutes of Shevchenko leaving, a third of the class had made the same Olympic sprint to the bathroom.

As yet another kid walked up to grab a gummy, Janet called, "Wait! Don't touch that bear!" We all looked at her like the crazy girl she could be. "I think it's the gummies. Only the people who have eaten them have made a run for the bathrooms."

The kid at the desk slowly backed away and went back to her seat.

The funny thing was that most people figured Mr. Shev must have dusted them with something as a way of punishing anyone who tried to steal them. Like we were rats and the gummies his poisonous cheese. And that his plan had backfired.

"Did you guys get that email from that Revenger guy?" Blake asked from across the room.

"I thought it was a joke," someone else said. "Do you think the Revenger could have done this?"

"I don't think diarrhea is going to get rid of Mr. Shev," Blake said. "But maybe."

"Well, whatever this Revenger guy is up to, if it gets rid of Shevchenko I'll donate some money to him," someone else said.

As the class talked about how great this new Revenger would be to get rid of Mr. Shev, Marcus held his fist out to me, and I bumped it with mine. It was only after I did it that I realized Janet was staring at us. I could practically see the wheels turning in her mind, putting the pieces together.

A second later she mouthed, "What did you guys do?"

CHAPTER 6

"Nothing, I swear," I lied.

The bell for recess sounded. Before we could get outside, Janet cornered us in the back of the class. Everyone else headed out to the playground.

"I know you two did something. You're responsible somehow."

"You heard everyone," Marcus said. "It was that Revenger guy."

"Just stop," Janet said. "You can't fool me. Catching a wild animal and taking him home to his owner is one thing. But making a teacher and a bunch of kids sick is another."

"We already told you," I said. "We're not the Revenger."

When we had Evil Cat at the vet, Janet showed up asking a lot of questions. We didn't admit to anything but made a deal with her—we introduced her to her new idol, Gunner Tensdale, in exchange for her keeping her mouth shut about seeing us.

It must've been Janet's years of listening to gossip that somehow sharpened her lie-detecting skills. I was determined to keep her from figuring out that Marcus and I were the Revengers.

I was about to launch into a new level of denial when she said something I hadn't expected. "I want to help."

"Huh?" Marcus and I said in the same breath.

She put her hands on her hips. "Do you know how many detentions I've had in my life?"

I figured it must've been a low number so I guessed, "A dozen?"

"Zero," she snapped. "Not a single one. Not until that jerk came here. I want him gone. I want Ms. Blindly back. But if she's not coming back for a while, I want a different sub."

I think I just sat there blinking for a while. Luckily Marcus managed to gather his thoughts enough to reply. "Well it's not us. If you want to be involved I say donate money to them."

Her eyes narrowed. "You know more than you're saying." She chewed her lip waiting for us to say something. When we didn't she said, "Fine, play it that way. But I think you know them, and I want you to give them a message." We kept quiet and she rolled her eyes before continuing. "Tell them that diarrhea stunt better not have been their best work. Because if it is, they'll never make it. Total amateur hour, if you ask me." She stepped closer and said, "Remember. He's from Kiev." She turned and left the classroom.

We kept a low profile over recess and agreed that Janet was right. We needed to do something better. Something really smart. If we weren't smarter we'd just make Shevchenko angry and he'd direct his anger at the easiest possible targets: us.

When we got back from recess, Shevchenko and Principal Rathers stood at the front of the room. Mr. Shev couldn't even stand up straight—he had one hand on the desk and the other gripping his stomach. His face was still a bit green around his mouth and eyes, but an angry red tinged his cheeks.

"Who is responsible?" He glared around the room at those of us who hadn't eaten the gummies. Another spasm must have hit his stomach because he gave a pained grunt. When no one spoke, he gathered himself up and took a step toward the door. "Fine. Don't say a word. I'll discover who is responsible. Faceless criminals don't stay faceless for long."

He shuffled awkwardly down the aisle, pausing every few steps before continuing through the door. Principal Rathers waited until the door closed behind our substitute before he stepped up to the class. "This might have seemed like a prank," he began, his voice serious. "But it went too far. If anyone here is responsible, please come see me in my office. Same goes for anyone who thinks they might have an idea about this." He looked around the room at each of us like he was trying to find the guilt in someone's eyes. I turned my gaze firmly to my desk. "I'm going to need you all to go to the library for the next hour or so. Mr. Shevchenko is confident he'll be ready to take control of the class again in just a short while."

Once we were in the library, Marcus whispered to me, "I can't wait to see how this plays out." We sat in the middle of a bank of computers, away from the rest of the class. "You heard

Shev in there, right? It's like a game to him now—or at least a challenge he can't back away from."

"I'm not worried about him outsmarting us," I said. "All paths lead to the Revengers, and that's a dead end. We need to not worry about Shev catching us, and instead we need to worry that we're going to blow this opportunity. What we need is a new plan. Something nonphysical, something ingenious— something that will prove once and for all that we're not to be underestimated. No job too big. You know what I'm saying?"

"I know the goal, but maybe his horribleness is impervious to the Revengers' brand of karma," Marcus said.

"No, it's not. He's not. We just need to think outside the box." Turning to the computer, I did an online search. Something Mr. Shev had said kept rattling around in my head and I could feel the start of a big idea forming in my mind. Just a hint of one, and I didn't want to waste any time. "Where did Janet say he was from?"

"You know I don't listen to her when she's babbling," Marcus said.

"No, think. We know he's from Ukraine, but what city? I know he's mentioned it."

"Oh, you're right! It's... Key-ette?" Marcus said. "Something like "Key-ette, or Key—something."

"Kiev!" I said, nearly shouting. "That's it, Kiev. Yes."

Marcus shrugged. "Okay. And why is that important?"

"Hang on. I have an idea."

Beside me, Marcus rocked back and forth in his chair. I would have told him to stop, but a quick glance around the library showed most of my classmates doing the same thing, so I didn't say anything.

I followed a few more links and checked a few more sites before I found what I was looking for. "Yes," I whispered. "I knew I'd find something." I sent myself an email with what I'd found and Marcus leaned over my shoulder to read the webpage.

"I don't get it," he said.

I leaned close to Marcus and whispered the plan.

He sat back and scratched the back of his head. "Dude, that's... that's genius."

"It might be."

"Might be?" Marcus shook his head. "No, man, it is totally genius."

"Unless it goes too far and people track us down. If that happens—if they figure out who the Revengers really are, we're finished."

CHAPTER 7

Everyone who ate a gummy bear went home sick. The one exception was Mr. Shev, who toughed it out somehow. He called us all back to class about forty minutes after we'd gone to the library. Except for a few quick departures from the class in the middle of lectures, he held it together pretty well. He kept watching everyone in the class really carefully though, and taking notes. I think he was trying to get one of us to crack under the pressure of his stare. No one did. No one mentioned the Revenger email either. It might have been wishful thinking, but it seemed everyone was hopeful that the mystery Revenger would come through for them.

We would.

Shevchenko cancelled the day's detentions. He said half the people who had detention weren't there anyway, but from the way he shifted from one foot to the other we knew he wanted to leave right away. His blue Honda Civic tore out of the parking lot about the same time Marcus and I walked across the front lawn. Not having detention meant we had a chance to get the rest of our plan sorted out.

It wasn't going to be easy. There were a lot of moving parts that had to come together just right. If it didn't, the whole thing would blow up in our faces. Since we planned to get him out of our lives forever, without actually hurting the guy, there was really only one option. I mean, he had mentioned how much he wanted to visit his homeland again. We were essentially doing him a favor. I felt a smile creep onto my face. If we pulled this off we were going to be legends.

At its core, the plan was simple: We were going to get Shevchenko deported.

We bought supplies from the craft store using some of the money we'd earned on our first mission—Evil Cat. Back at my place, we began to put the pieces together. As we did, I became more and more certain we were onto something incredible. A business venture that was going to make us rich and famous... anonymously famous, if that were possible. We created an album filled with stories we found online of one of Ukraine's most notorious criminals, Boris Jovanosvski. He was known for bank heists, racketeering, money laundering, and evading police for almost thirty years. No one even knew what he looked like, though he had continued to rob banks every few years.

We used different types of paper, different ink, even different pairs of scissors to trim the pages. Once we had most of the pages filled, we aged it by tossing it in the oven for a couple minutes. Then we dragged it behind our bikes a short distance, and stomped on it. When it looked sufficiently old, we shoved it into my backpack so we wouldn't forget to take it to school the next day.

Then we used an online translation service to turn one crucial sentence into Ukrainian. On a message board for people looking for tips on traveling to Kiev—Ukraine's capital city— Marcus asked one of the members to check our translation and adjust it to something more natural sounding. Marcus wrote it out in the proper Ukrainian alphabet, which looked a lot like upside down letters and sharp, squared lines.

Now we were ready for the next part of our plan.

Marcus downloaded a new video app for his phone, which his parents had recently bought for him, and we were set. We'd used almost all the money in the Revenger account, but we had a plan that was going to work. We knew it—okay, we were hopeful and confident. But the plan wasn't just good, it was genius-good. If we pulled it off the business was going to go viral.

Sitting back, Marcus glanced at me. "If this doesn't work and somehow the government gets involved and tracks us down—"

"We'll probably be finishing school in juvenile detention centers." I swallowed the lump in my throat.

"It's going to work," he said.

I held out my fist and he bumped it with his.

"Darn right it's going to." And I crossed my fingers behind my back for luck.

CHAPTER 8

We did have to do one or two slightly illegal things to set our plan into action—we had to sneak into school before it opened and we had to break into Mr. Shev's car—but neither one of those felt like crimes because we weren't taking anything, we were leaving something. If we were criminals, so was Santa Claus. Okay, I was probably stretching with that one, but thinking it helped.

First, I had to ditch Sky—she couldn't go to school that early, and there wasn't a chance we would let her tag along while we planted incriminating evidence on our teacher.

I told Mom that Marcus and I were going in early to work on a project—which wasn't a lie—and asked if Ronie would walk Sky to school. Mom agreed without a second thought, although Sky pouted, her bottom lip stuck out, about not getting to go in with us.

"Don't be mad," I told her. "We'll hang out after school. I'll make you popcorn with extra butter."

"Promise?" she asked.

"Promise," I said. *If we don't get arrested.*

Once we got to school, we staked out the park across from the teachers' parking lot. Only a few cars stood idle in the lot. If Janet was here she'd know whose car was whose. But I didn't see a blue Honda Civic—the kind of car Mr. Shev drove—which meant he wasn't here yet. I figured we were good to go.

We crept up to the side door of the school, hoping it would be unlocked. I rattled the handle. It was bolted shut.

"Great," Marcus whispered, looking around for teachers coming in early. "Now what?"

"I know the back door is open. The basketball team is practicing in the gym, so if we go that way at least thirty people will see us. That leaves us with one other option."

Marcus slowly turned back to me. "You don't mean...?"

"Yeah. Front door break-in."

We crept along the side of the building like true burglars. Marcus worked as a lookout. When we got to the double doors of the main entrance, I reached out to try one door. Locked. The other opened with a soft *click*.

We slid through the door but Marcus didn't catch it on the close and it banged shut with a ring that echoed through the empty hallway. We both froze. Someone was in this building— the cars outside proved it. What if they'd heard the noise? When no one appeared, we started down the hall. We could see lights on inside the main office. I leaned forward to peek into the doorway. Ms. Kim sat at a desk, working at her computer. She sat with her side to us, so hopefully we could slip past the doorway without her seeing us. We had to be quick, though.

I motioned to Marcus to wait. Another quick peek and I darted across the doorway. My stomach jumped up to my throat as if it wanted to strangle me for doing this. I'd need to get better nerves if I was going to keep up this Revenger business.

Working as lookout for Marcus, I watched as Ms. Kim turned her back to get some files. I waved for him to dash across. Once he made it safely to the other side, we both let out a sigh. Turning, we hurried down the hall.

We finally made it to our classroom and ducked inside. Up at the board I wrote the Ukrainian sentence while Marcus held up the paper to make sure the characters were right. It was with that weird alphabet. Almost as hard as copying a picture.

When we had it done, I stood back and looked at it.

Я Борис Jovanovski, але ви ніколи не будете це довести.

We pulled the world map over top of the sentence and were just about to sneak back out when we heard a clunk from down the hall.

Easing forward, I glanced around the corner of the doorway. The janitor rolled a cart of supplies into the bathroom down the hall. Supplies that included a plunger. Poor guy. I didn't even want to imagine the horror he had to face after the gummy-bear incident.

We waited until he went inside the guys' bathroom, then hustled back down the hall. We stopped for another look into the office doorway, then dashed across and out the front door to freedom. Sprinting across the parking lot, we kept going until we hit the bushes on the other side. Crashing down on the grass, I let out a wheezing breath.

"Oh, man," Marcus said between gasps for air. "If we keep this business up I'm going to need heart medication. My chest is pounding."

Mine was too, but we'd done it. "Our plan is falling into place." I rolled upright. "But we still have a long way to go."

Eventually Shevchenko's blue Honda pulled into the lot. He marched into the school, his face gray and set into a grimace.

He looked a couple of pounds lighter.

Marcus had downloaded a tutorial for how to break into Shevchenko's car with a coat hanger and one of those wooden wedges you use to keep a door open, but when we crept up to the car I saw the passenger window was down just enough for me to reach through and unlock the door. Once we got it open, Marcus popped open the trunk. I pulled out the album we'd made and tucked it beside his spare tire.

"At least that part was easy," Marcus said.

When it was finally time to head into class, we strolled in as if we weren't in the midst of pulling off our biggest job yet.

Marcus handled the last step. He kept his phone in his hand. We had to record what happened next or the whole plan would be wasted.

After the morning bell rang and we were all in our seats, Mr. Shev looked around the room, his arms folded. "Just a reminder to those of you who had detention yesterday—you will make it up today with extra time."

Several people groaned.

"Now let's look at chapter four in your history book." He walked to the chalkboard, muttering something about the map being in his way. He tugged the bottom and the map rolled back up onto itself. When he saw the sentence he froze.

Janet's hand went up, but Mr. Shev erased the sentence before turning around and seeing Janet.

"What is it?" he asked.

"What did that say?"

He smiled. "It was written in Ukrainian and it said, 'I am Boris Jovanosvski, but you'll never prove it.'"

Janet straightened at her desk.

Someone else in the room asked, "You speak Ukrainian?"

Shevchenko let out a slow frustrated sigh. "I sometimes wonder if you kids hear a word I say. I *am* Ukrainian." Shevchenko pointed across the room. "One day detention for speaking out of turn, and another day for not remembering where I was born, *despite* the fact that I did a whole unit on the country just last year with this class."

"Who's Boris Jovanosvki?" another kid asked from near the front of the class — after putting up their hand and being called on by Shev.

"He's a pretty infamous criminal where I'm from. He's a gangster, kind of. Not someone you'd want to meet if he didn't like you." He narrowed his eyes and scanned the room. "Whoever wrote that must've thought it would be funny to compare me to a ruthless criminal. Frankly, I'm not offended. When I was growing up Jovanosvki had a reputation like Robin Hood. A man of the people."

"Is he in jail?"

Shev shrugged. "I wouldn't know. Ukrainian news isn't that big over here."

The conversation progressed that way for the next few minutes. Students took turns asking Shev about Ukraine and he answered with an almost enthusiastic tone. He liked talking about where he was from. He even talked about how he'd long wanted to raise awareness of Ukrainian tourism and how it had been so long since he last saw his family. It almost made me feel good about our plan. If we pulled it off he'd see them soon enough.

Another hand shot up and another student said, "Can you say something in Ukrainian?"

He turned and the corner of his mouth twitched. He was totally into this. The fact that he spoke two languages made him pretty impressive, at least in his eyes. "Sure, I'll tell you what that sentence said." He stared out at the class and said the words carefully. The only part I understood was when he said the name Boris Jovanosvski but that was enough to know our plan had worked—at least stage one had. I turned to Marcus. He gave me a nod, smiled, and slipped his phone into his pocket.

CHAPTER 9

We made the call at lunch hour. The phone line only rang twice before someone picked up. "Hello, this is Crimestoppers. My name is Wendy. Is there something you'd like to report?"

"Hi, Wendy," I said confidently. "There sure is. We've found a wanted criminal and have video to prove it."

They came after school—during detention while Mr. Shev had us at the board working out math problems. Not just a couple of officers, but a whole team. There must've been twenty cars screeching to a stop outside, and when they burst through the door, assault rifles drawn, shouting for everyone to get down, all the color in Shevchenko's face—what little was left from yesterday's gummy adventure—vanished. They grabbed him, threw him against the chalkboard, and cuffed his hands behind his back.

"Boris Jovanosvski, you're under arrest."

"What is the meaning of this?" he said, his voice shaking. "I demand you remove these things from my hands!"

"Not until we're downtown, buddy," the arresting officer said.

We watched, mouths open, as they patted him down. When they pulled Mr. Shev away with a jerk of his arm, Marcus grinned at me. My gaze landed on Janet. She stared at me, eyes narrowed. Slowly a grin spread over her face. She nodded her head. I felt my smile widen. "Bravo," she mouthed while giving me a golf clap. "Bravo."

It wasn't just local news that showed up with vans the following day. News vans from all over the country packed all the parking lots. Some international. The notorious criminal Boris Jovanosvski had finally been caught after years of evading and escaping police.

The album we had created looked like a trophy book, detailing every crime he'd ever committed.

We knew that eventually they'd discover Mr. Shev wasn't really Jovanosvski, but we found out the Ukrainian government had pulled some strings and had Shevchenko flown to Kiev that night so they could authenticate if he was Boris. It would have been a huge win for them, but of course he wasn't a criminal. Still, we got to say we had one of our targets deported to the Ukraine, which was way bigger than sending Ronie's boyfriend,

Gunner, off to L.A.

It was only a couple days after the deportation that news came out that they'd gotten the wrong man. Mr. Shev was exonerated, as they called it—which meant he was freed with a lot of apologies. According to the news report, he received two million apologies—in the form of dollars—from the US government for the arrest and deportation.

He stopped by the class a couple weeks later and looked like a new man. He was smiling and looked pretty sharp in a suit that fit so perfectly it looked like it was made especially for him.

Ms. Blindly was back then and she stood beside him, with her usual smile. "The school board wanted to bring Mr. Shevchenko back to see you kids so you didn't worry. I know many of you witnessed what happened when he was arrested and we thought seeing him again would help put some closure on the situation. We don't want any of you to worry."

Mr. Shev cleared his throat. "As Ms. Blindly said, I'm only back to say that there are no hard feelings about what happened here a couple weeks ago," Shev said. "Believe it or not, getting deported was the best thing that could've happened."

"Are you going to be our substitute again?" Janet asked. She didn't put up her hand and spoke so abruptly it was almost like she was trying to show the man that she'd purposely spoken out of turn.

Mr. Shev grinned like he knew exactly what she'd done and didn't care anymore. "No, I'm leaving my teaching position—at least for now. I have plans to explore some other options."

"Now that you're rich," someone said.

Shev smiled. "Who knows, maybe I'll come back to teaching in a couple years and our paths will cross again."

You better hope not, I thought.

Marcus and I hit the paintball park after school, but the whole way there he didn't say a word.

"What's wrong with you?" I asked as we geared up.

"He's better off," Marcus said, stepping into his coveralls. "Once again the Revengers take a target out and they're better off for it. I mean, the guy's a millionaire now. A millionaire."

"He's not coming back," I said. "He'll never be a teacher again. We did that. We got a guy deported. Have you seen the number of hits we've received on our website?"

"Of course I have. I'm the one who had to explain to my dad why the server keeps crashing."

"And our Revenger bank account isn't exactly hurting either," I said. "With a few more jobs we'll be able to take the month-long spy course next summer."

"I know. I just want people to see us as ruthless, man. I want Revenger to be a word people whisper. Like, oh no, the Revengers are coming."

"Like the bogeyman?"

"Exactly like the bogeyman."

"Well the bogeyman's not real, and we are. Give it some time, man. We're starting out and we've just knocked one out of the park. I'm totally thrilled about it."

He held out his arms. "What about paintball? Do you really think it's necessary? I'm not loving this game."

"It's good practice, dude. We used the stalking skills we learned here to sneak into the school. Trust me, we need to keep it up."

"Fine, but only if you'll stand there and let me shoot you twice to start."

"You bet," I said. He nodded and we headed to the gun area of the park. Thing is, Marcus wanted us to be scarier, and that meant I didn't have to keep that promise about standing still while he shot me. As soon as I loaded my gun, he was getting two to the stomach.

After all, Revengers play by their own rules.

Keep reading for an extended

Sneak Peek at *BOOK #3*

in the

REVENGER SERIES

CHAPTER 1

*T*hree... two... one...

"Now!" Marcus said.

Nothing happened. Marcus groaned. Three seconds later the fire alarm went off in the flower shop across the street.

"I need to work on my timing." Marcus nodded at the store across the street from us. "Other than that—one more job completed." He dusted off his hands.

Just then, Mr. Lee jogged out of the store, soaked and red-in-the-face angry with a bunch of roses in his hand, holding them up like a sword for battle.

"I can't believe that worked." I took a step back into the shadows of the alley. "The things you can learn these days from the internet, right? I almost don't blame parents for trying to watch what their kids are doing online."

Marcus laughed. "I love it when my parents try to do that. They think that because they're good at computer stuff they can out-think me. Not likely. But speaking of useful stuff online, I'm putting together a new website all about hacking stuff. Not computer hacking, but like world hacking. Like how to wreak havoc in shopping centers, and..." he nodded toward the flower shop, "how to rig an industrial fire sprinkler to go off."

"I'll give you credit for the fire sprinkler," I said, "but what do you know about *wreaking havoc*? Who even says wreaking havoc?"

Marcus folded his arms. He'd been my best friend forever, and it was pretty much a draw as far as which of us got the other one into more trouble. But he was also my partner in our Revenger business. Essentially we were fixers—people came to us with problems and we fixed them. Have a crumby boss? A bully at school? A dog that bites you on your way to school? A sadistic teacher whose power-tripping is making your life miserable? We're the guys who can take care of those things— for a price.

Mr. Lee, it turned out, was a problem for a number of people. In fact, we'd received three requests to take him out. And the reasons behind two of the requests were clear as glass.

The first request was from a group of kids who wanted him to pay for selling them flowers that died really quick. Mother's Day presents, they'd said, that had wilted before they'd even had a chance to give them to their mothers. That request wasn't enough on its own. Mr. Lee's shop had a reputation for poor quality, and everyone knew it, so a bunch of kids probably weren't going to pay us much—if anything.

Marcus thought being a florist was reason enough to take him down. "A service to guys everywhere," he said, joking. "No more wasting money on things that cost a fortune and are born to die."

"I say wreaking havoc," Marcus said, "and we're pretty much experts on it. But I was going to get information from the net and compile it all into one mega site." He tugged at the collar of his t-shirt and fanned his face. "Hey, do you want me to make the hacker site part of our Revenger site? If we do it right it could be a kind of one-stop-shop for all things anarchy."

I shook my head. "Let's keep the Revenger site basic, okay? Just keep the form people fill out to tell us about their problem, and the button for payments. We don't want to add stuff that might get traced back to us."

"Traced back to us?" Marcus asked. "Trust me, that's not going to happen. Anyone digs into our site and they'll think we're from a really small town near Hong Kong."

I had no idea how in the world Marcus did what he did, and he always joked that I was clueless—but really, I was only clueless compared to Marcus. What I knew about computers was pretty much what any other eleven-year-old knew. Marcus just happened to be born into a house of computer experts. Plus, I was pretty sure he had a knack for them that went a bit beyond the stuff his parents taught him. He'd been making websites since he was old enough to grab a keyboard. His dad was a programmer and his mom worked in internet marketing. But despite having a whack of websites, only a couple of Marcus's sites had ever made him any money, and our Revenger site was quickly becoming the most popular. We had been saving the money for spy camp, but lately we'd shelved that plan and instead put the money back into our growing business.

He pointed at me. "Hey, what if we called ourselves Anarchy Revengers or Anarchy Revengers for Hire?"

"We're already the Revengers. We have a website and a logo and a slogan. Let's just leave it alone. Besides, how are you going to pull all the stuff from all those sites into one place? Won't it take you forever?"

He shrugged. "It's not going to be that tough. I created a bot that mines content from like a million different sites and then I'll probably use another bot to make sense of that information. It could be pretty cool. Even if we don't use it on our site I'll bet there'll be a lot we can use for the jobs we get hired for."

"Actually," I said, "that does sound like a good idea."

A fire truck rolled up a minute later. The firefighters jumped into action. They pulled out hoses and stuff, but since there wasn't actually a fire two of them ran around to the side of the building, no doubt looking for the water shutoff valve.

A couple of other firefighters went inside. A minute later they came out and gestured for Mr. Lee to come back into the store too.

"Wow, that was faster than we thought it'd be," I said. "Do you think the water was even on long enough?"

"Dunno. It's not like I'm an expert on flowers. But I killed my mom's fern when I overwatered it. Must be the same for orchids and roses and daisies and whatever else he has in there."

I tried to sink even deeper into the shade. I kind of wished I'd been in the store when the sprinkler had come on just so I could cool down a bit.

Marcus wiped the sweat off his face with the bottom of his shirt. "Let's just see what happens."

The second request we received to target Mr. Lee really brought the florist into our crosshairs. A genuine request from an adult. It was simple. It was direct. And it was from a woman named Deloris. She was newly married and claimed Mr. Lee ruined her wedding. She filled out our online form with three simple sentences that read:

This jerk ruined my wedding by bringing flowers to the reception that died before it started. He has no business being a florist. I will pay—gladly—to see him get what he deserves. —Deloris M.

She'd followed the instructions we posted and uploaded a photo as well as the street address for Mr. Lee's Flower Garden. Mr. Lee's small downtown shop had a sign announcing his store had a "focus on freshness." Yeah, right.

Our reputation had made it to the ears of adults, and we couldn't wait to prove ourselves.

Our fire-sprinkler sabotage was the first part of our plan. There was a chance, we thought, that the sprinkler would be enough—that we'd have caused enough damage to shut the place down. It would serve as a message, an example of what we could do. Show everyone the Revengers weren't do-gooders. We were ruthless. Sure we only took jobs we believed in—jobs taking down people we believed deserved to be taken down—but we wanted our reputation to speak for itself. And we wanted clients to know one thing: once we accepted a job, we were in it to win it.

Turned out, though, that the first part of our plan wasn't enough. Not even close.

Fifteen minutes after the alarm went off, the firefighters were already packing up their gear. I nudged Marcus. We walked casually toward the strip mall and joined the onlookers who were being held back by the firefighters. We slipped between people and slowly made our way through the crowd to where yellow tape flapped. Mr. Lee stood talking to one of the firefighters.

"A faulty sprinkler head?" Mr. Lee waved a hand out. "I didn't even know those things could be faulty."

The firefighter removed his helmet and rubbed the back of his neck. His fire jacket hung open, unzipped, and he looked like he wanted to go back into the flower shop and start that sprinkler again to cool off.

"Oh, sure. I've seen it before. I suggest having all the sprinkles checked by professionals. If they're not installed right they can go off during heat waves like we've been having this past week." The firefighter looked at the building and shook his head. "To tell you the truth, what happened in there is almost one of those happy accidents, what do they call that? There's a word for it I think...?"

"Serendipity," Mr. Lee grumbled.

"Yeah, that's it. I mean, you have a store that's essentially built to handle water spills—large drains, tiled floors, rubber baseboards. The only sprinkler that went off was in the middle of the store, right over the bulk of your stock. I'm no gardener, but I bet your flowers have been feeling the effects of the city's water restrictions. They'll probably be better off thanks to your inside rain."

Mr. Lee's shoulders slumped and he glared at his own shop. "Yeah, I guess you're right."

Serendipity wasn't a word I'd known before, but we weren't trying to give Mr. Lee any happy accidents.

In the end, it was the third request that sealed the deal. It just made our target too interesting to pass up. We were already formulating a plan to take the guy down because we were confident Angry Bride would pay up if we really got the guy good. But when we got the third request, well, the stakes rose to a whole other level. That request was from someone who wanted the shop closed down once and for all and it came from someone we'd never have expected—Mr. Lee himself. The guy actually wanted himself to be taken out.

We didn't know why, but we were happy to oblige.

CHAPTER 2

*O*ur sprinkler sabotage was a massive failure. Not only had it *not* destroyed the stock, or the store, the firefighter had basically said our intervention actually made it possible for the florist to get around the water restrictions the city was dishing out. His flowers were probably going to be the best in town.

I decided before the trucks rolled away from the scene that we'd leave that particular part out when we posted the job-specks on our website.

We shook off the bust and launched immediately into the next phase of our plan—that included learning everything we could about the target, and it was an excellent opportunity to test our stalking skills.

Tall and super thin, Mr. Lee reminded me of a metal fence pole. That made following him pretty easy. We weren't sure how old he was, but we figured he had to be a few years older than my dad. In his fifties maybe. One of our goals was to know everything about the people we targeted. We planned on having files on everyone, but so far our file on Mr. Lee was paper-thin. We didn't even have any idea why he'd put the target on himself. All his email to us said was, "I want my flower shop to be taken out."

"We should actually call her Angry Bride," Marcus said.

"What do you mean?" Mr. Lee had closed his shop about the same time the fire trucks left, and went for a walk. We'd been following him for over an hour. He'd gone home—which, it turned out, wasn't far from his shop—and changed out of his wet clothes. He stopped at a drugstore and bought a pack of breath mints. As we followed him, his pace had doubled as if he was running late.

I was tired and sweaty and I couldn't decide if the heat or Marcus's stupid comments bothered me more.

Marcus swiped at the sweat on his forehead. "I mean, Angry Bride can be the code name for Deloris. Plus, it sounds like we're saying Angry Bird, so even if someone does hear us, they'll think we're talking about the game."

I blinked. "Um... I think you're overthinking this. No one is listening to us, and if we said Deloris or Angry Bride, or Deloris the Angry Bride, it wouldn't matter. But if you're worried about it, maybe just keep your mouth shut when we're around other people."

"Oh, people are listening, Jared." He made a scene of turning in a slow, dramatic circle. He dropped his voice to a whisper. "People are always listening."

"Give me a break."

"We need code names," he said in his normal voice. "And they should be cool like—" Suddenly, he grabbed my arm and pulled me off the sidewalk and behind a tree. I thought he was still playing up the drama of his code-name idea so I smacked his hand away. But he gestured up ahead and it didn't look like he was kidding, so I turned.

Mr. Lee had stopped on the street corner. My mind went to the recreation center that wasn't far from where we were, and the park with shade-giving trees, or better yet the giant indoor pool filled with cool water. I crossed my fingers and hoped Mr. Lee was headed there. He checked his phone and started walking again, his pace even faster than before.

"Who do you think he's meeting?" Marcus asked as we started after him again.

I shrugged. "I don't care as long as we figure out a good way to take him out. I know our sprinkler plan was supposed to be phase one, but we hadn't meant to make his business better.

Besides, if the man *wants* to be targets of the Revengers, the least we could do is make it quick."

Sweat dripped down my back. We rounded the corner just in time to see him duck into the rec center.

"Hurry," I said, feeling a sudden rush of excitement. "Air-conditioning awaits."

We burst through the doors and into a blast of cold air. Marcus shivered and I closed my eyes for a second as the cool relief washed over me. When I opened them I saw Mr. Lee at the far end of the lobby, heading toward the stairs that led to the second floor. I knew the building well, and the second level had a big deck that overlooked the pool and a large food-court style cafeteria. Mr. Lee towered over the other people. From the way folks were hanging out it seemed like most everyone had come here just to escape the heat. We didn't need to be so worried about being seen now—there were loads of kids our age wandering around. We followed Mr. Lee up the stairs and realized all at once why he'd come.

The restaurants on the second floor were situated against the back wall, with tables and chairs filling the rest of the space all the way to a curved glass wall that looked out over the indoor pool. Today, however, a large section of the room—nearly half— had been sectioned off with rope. Every table in that section had a woman sitting alone with a pencil and what looked like a score card—like the kind you'd use on a mini-golf course.

"Speed dating," Marcus said, pointing to a large sign that

said just that. The sign had an image of a clock and said, *Matched in a Minute!*

Mr. Lee stepped up to a table near an opening to the roped section. He said something to the man at the table and then picked up a sticker name badge and pressed it to his chest. Then he joined the dozen or so other men waiting. Some of the guys shifted their weight nervously; others glanced around like they were worried someone would see them. A few looked normal—like Mr. Lee—but most of the men leered at the women like hungry animals.

"And this is voluntary?" I asked.

Marcus pointed across the room to a table on the non-dating side. It stood close enough to the roped-off area that we'd be able to hear some of what was being said at a few of the dating tables.

I grabbed a seat and Marcus grabbed some fries and two Cokes from one of the food counters. When he came back a bell rang and guys started heading out to various tables. At the table closest to us sat a serious-looking woman.

She looked like a librarian from the movies—hair pulled back in a tight bun, glasses over her small eyes, sour mouth pulled down, and a stuffy all-business kind of coat and skirt and buttoned-up shirt. When the conversation began it was clear she intended to use her sixty seconds to the fullest. The way she grilled the guys that landed at her table you'd have thought she was interrogating them for suspected criminal activity. I felt a bit sorry for the guys, but grateful we'd managed to get close enough to hear the conversations.

The bell rang again and all the guys swapped seats. Mr. Lee took a seat a couple tables away from Ms. Librarian. It wouldn't be long before we'd hear how he fared against the woman.

"What do you do?" Ms. Librarian asked.

The guy who'd just come over to her table hadn't even had a chance to sit down. "Oh, um, I, um, I work in finance. What about you?"

"HR. Kids?"

"Um, none yet." The poor guy glanced at his watch and looked around like maybe sixty seconds was going to be too long a time with Ms. HR-Librarian.

She gave him a tired look. "So then you do want some?"

"Why? Are you looking to sell a few?" He laughed and seemed to see she hadn't even cracked a smile.

"Man," Marcus whispered. "This is painful."

The questions went on like that—rapid fire—until the bell rang again. All the guys stood and shuffled to the next table.

There were two more rounds before Mr. Lee landed at Ms. HR-Librarian's table.

"I'm Andrew," he said and put out his hand to shake hers.

She stared at his hand like he'd offered her a snake. "What do you do, Andrew?" She didn't say her own name.

Mr. Lee smiled. "I have a flower shop. What about you?"

"HR," she said, the words clipped. She narrowed her eyes even more and pushed her glasses up on her nose. "You don't look like a florist."

Mr. Lee shifted in his chair and asked, "What does a florist look like?"

I was surprised how calm he sounded and how confident he looked. Ms. HR-Librarian reminded me too much of Mr. Shevchenko, a substitute teacher we'd had at school who could terrify anyone in any class. I wouldn't want to be sitting with her.

She shrugged. "Have you always wanted to be a florist?"

Mr. Lee shook his head. "Have you always wanted to be in HR?"

"It seemed the obvious choice." She tapped the tip of her pen on the table. "I'm a people person."

Marcus choked on a fry and started coughing like he was dying. I thumped him on the back and tried to block him from everyone's stare. A second later, Marcus got it under control.

"I inherited the place," Mr. Lee said. "It was my dad's, and he passed a few years ago and I just sort of landed in it. I'm not quite as drawn to the business as he was."

"So you're, what? Honor bound to run the place? You don't have a choice."

"Something like that."

"And if you weren't? What would you do then?"

Mr. Lee smiled. "There was a time I thought I'd make a decent travel writer." He glanced up at the ceiling as if seeing something other than white tiles and air ducts. "I loved to imagine visiting all kinds of exotic locations." Sitting up, he looked hopeful for a moment and asked, "Have you done any traveling?"

"Outside of the country?" Her mouth tightened and she tapped her pen again. "No, thank you. That's never interested me. If it's what you want to do, why aren't you doing it?"

"I suppose I'd need a reason to leave the shop. An excuse to close the family business I run with my brother and his son."

"Such as love?" the woman asked.

Mr. Lee shrugged. "More like a fire." He opened his mouth to ask another question, but the bell rang.

The woman kept her head down over her score card. Mr. Lee gave her a nod and shuffled to the next table. I looked at Marcus as the next unlucky soul took a seat across from the woman with no name.

Marcus smiled and shoved a fry in his mouth. "At least we know why he wants out. And what's more, he's given us a great idea for how to do it."

"What? You mean a fire?" I shook my head. "He was joking."

"Was he?"

After draining my Coke, I rattled the ice in the drink cup. "We just finished trying to kill all his stock with water. We're not going to turn around and burn his place down."

Marcus's mouth curved up in an evil grin. "Aren't we?"

CHAPTER 3

After we'd stepped out of the rec center and back into a wall of heat—a guy can only take so much speed dating—Marcus turned to me.

"Okay, I agree we shouldn't burn his store down. But Mr. Lee wants out. That's the key. That's how we take him out. Angry Bride gets what she wants, the people of this city get a bad flower guy gone, and he gets what he wants."

"I thought you were against missions where everyone ended up happy? And would you please stop calling her Angry Bride?"

"That's her code name." He grinned. "And I'm not against someone getting what they want as long as it works with what we want too. I just don't want jerks to leave happy. And I don't think this guy is a jerk anymore. A dork, totally. Not the best florist, sure. But not a jerk. I mean, you heard him—he inherited the place. He feels like he has to keep it."

We spent the walk home working out possible ways to destroy the man's business without destroying the man—or committing illegal acts of arson. We thought of some great ones too. Buying a crate of termites and releasing them into his walls.

But it wasn't easy to find a place where you could buy termites by the crate and besides, they'd take forever. We thought about throwing some rats into his shop and calling the health department. But it was a flower shop, not a restaurant. We scratched that idea when we decided that was nothing a few traps wouldn't solve, anyway. In the end, Marcus came up with the best plan. But he didn't think of it until after we made it back to his house and our brains were half melted from the heat.

Sitting in Marcus's room, eating ice cream and surfing the net on Marcus's tablet, Marcus said, "What if we just made it so Mr. Lee was forced to take a break from flowers? I mean, it's risky. He might just come back and start again, but what if we force him to close his shop for a few weeks? We could give him the chance to have an adventure and if that sparks him into being a travel writer he'll just sell his business." He looked at me with a huge smile. "What do you think?"

"I think I don't even know your plan and you're smiling like a fat kid who just found a cookie. C'mon already. Spill."

"We flood the place," Marcus said. He held up his hand as if he wanted a high five for coming up with the idea. I groaned, and he quickly added, "Not a crazy flood. I'm not saying we turn the place into a swimming pool."

I threw up my hands. "Again? We already tried that, and it didn't work. Now you're saying we need to try it again but worse? What, do you propose we sabotage all the sprinkler heads in the store, not just one?" I didn't let Marcus reply before I added, "We need to be smarter. We need to think outside the box on this one."

Marcus shifted on his chair. He stirred his ice cream. He liked it best when it was melted. "Okay. What if we just kill all his plants with weed killer?" When I didn't say anything he added, "You hate it, don't you?"

"Yeah, well, whatever can kill plants might kill a person too. Look, what we need is a way for us to look ruthless, for Mr. Lee to experience something that puts him back on track to being a travel writer. He needs to decide to leave the flower shop on his own—or at least think the decision is his own."

"What do you suggest," Marcus asked. "Start a travel blog for him? Or maybe we get someone to buy all his plants and flowers? If he doesn't have anything to sell maybe that's when he'll decide he has to get into a new business?"

"Those aren't awful ideas," I said.

"Yes," Marcus said. "They are. They're truly awful. We need a win like we had with Shevchenko."

Shevchenko, or Mr. Shev as we used to call him, had been one of our first jobs. We'd gotten rid of him by making it look like he was a wanted criminal from Ukraine and he was deported. It was some of our finest work. It worked out well for him in the end since he's happier being back home, but we didn't advertise that.

Marcus must've read something in my face because he added, "Okay, so we didn't *really* destroy Shevchenko, but he's not teaching anymore is he? S   point goes to us. We're getting really good at this. And I still think we're on the right track with the key being to reignite Mr. Lee's inner adventurer. He seemed really excited when he talked about being a travel writer."

I put down my empty bowl and stood up. "Okay. Let's take the evening. After dinner we re-group and come up with an idea. I'll call you after dinner. We'll think of something awesome."

"We'd better—or we may just have to stop calling ourselves Revengers and start calling ourselves the Dream Makers. And that's *not* who we want to be."

CHAPTER 4

My dad's car was in the driveway when I walked up. The trunk was open and as I got closer I realized there were two small suitcases inside.

"Mom?" I called as I stepped through the door. My sister Ronie came careening around a corner and we nearly smashed into each other. At the last second she pivoted and spun like quarterback. She dumped her duffle bag at the door.

"You're in trouble," she said, almost singing the words. She flashed a snarky grin that said she knew something I didn't. She saw the flower in my hand I'd picked up outside Mr. Lee's and frowned. "That's not going to save you." She turned and bounded up the stairs two at a time to her room.

"Trouble," I said to myself. I tried to think of something I'd done that my folks wouldn't like. The only thing I could come up with was that they knew about the Revengers. A lump stuck in my throat and I couldn't swallow around it. I hoped Marcus hadn't been lazy about making sure the Internet fingerprint didn't lead back to either of us.

"Where have you been?" Mom practically yelled.

I jumped and looked up to see her standing in front of me. "W-with Marcus. Why?"

She breezed past me and called up the stairs, "Ronie, don't forget your jacket, dear. We'll likely go out tonight and it'll be cool." She turned back to me. "You're late." I must have given her a confused look because she said, "Remember, I told you I needed you home today to watch Sky until the sitter gets here."

My eyes widened. "I totally thought you were kidding."

"Jared!" She let out a long breath. "You knew we were going away for the night for Ronie's meet."

My sister had a gymnastics competition. I knew that. Since she'd gotten a fancy Russian coach she'd been killing it at competitions. That hadn't been the part I'd thought she'd been joking about. "I meant the babysitter. I thought you were joking about getting a sitter. I'm eleven, Mom. I think I can take care of myself for one night."

"And Sky?"

"Take her with you. She likes girl stuff. I'll be fine on my own."

Mom frowned at me. "We're not riding ponies and braiding hair, Jared. This is a big competition for your sister. It wouldn't be fun for Sky. Be here for Sky, okay?"

"Mom!" Ronie yelled, "Did you pack my shoes?"

"Yes, dear. They're already in the car." Mom slipped on her shoes and gave me a hug. "Your Aunt Rebecca will be here in a few minutes to babysit. She called to say she was on her way, just running a couple minutes late. But we have to get going if we're going to beat traffic out of the city."

Aunt Rebecca? I groaned. "Oh, c'mon! She's not even our real aunt." And she wasn't. She was just a close friend of my mom's who had always been called Aunt Rebecca. I hadn't learned the truth until I was eight. I'd felt totally cheated. I mean, who makes you call someone aunt who isn't your aunt? It wasn't right. But as soon as I found out she wasn't my real aunt I stopped feeling guilty about not liking her. Here's the thing about Aunt Rebecca: if there was a competition of safety challenges, she'd win it at the Olympics. *Cautious* wasn't a strong enough word to describe her.

I thought of one more way to get out of this and went for it. "Can we at least get a different sitter? Someone who didn't grow up during the last ice age?"

My mom gasped. "Ice age? We're the same age, I'll have you know."

Dad stepped into the foyer, smiling. "Ah, the ice age. It feels like just yesterday." He put his hand on my shoulder. "Did I ever tell you how I met your mom? It was the day of the great glacier melt and all the cave people came out for it. And there she was—"

Mom smacked his shoulder, smiling. "Don't you encourage him."

I held out my hands. "I only meant it would be nice if we could just have a normal babysitter sometimes. Or better yet, *no* babysitter."

"Sky loves her," my mom said. "And we trust she'll keep you both safe."

I turned to my dad, but he looked away, trying not to laugh. I knew what he was thinking because I was thinking the same thing. "Safe, Mom? Are you kidding? She's so safe she's actually un-safe. She once said the living room rug was dangerous because we could trip on the edge so she rolled it up and then Sky slipped on the hardwood floor. She nearly broke her neck!"

Mom cupped my chin and looked at me, her eyes soft and her mouth curving up a little. Her mind was made up. I wasn't going to change anything. "Be nice to her, Jared. She's like family to me. She should be like family to you."

Sky slipped around Mom and stuck herself to my side. She tucked her hand into mine and looked up at me with her huge green eyes. Her brown curls stuck up around her head. "I love Aunt Rebecca. She smells like cinnamon." Sky's voice practically dripped with sugar, like only a kid's voice her age could. I didn't have a chance.

"You know what else smells like cinnamon?" I muttered. "Zombies."

Sky gasped. "Aunt Rebecca's a zombie?"

My dad leveled a glare my direction and told Sky, "Your brother is just being silly. And you're right, Sky. Aunt Rebecca is perfectly lovable." He turned to me. "Jared, I expect you to help

Rebecca with Sky. It's been a while since she babysat you guys."

"Yeah. The last time was when I *was* a baby."

"It's just one night," Dad said. "Show us you can be grown up about this and maybe next time we need to go out we'll talk about letting you stay home alone." My mom cleared her throat. Dad glanced at her and looked back at me again. "We'll *talk* about it, understand?"

"But does it have to be Aunt Rebecca?" I said. "What about that person down the street—Rylee what's her name?" I knew exactly who Rylee was—Rylee Hottie Matthews. At sixteen she was the assistant captain of the cheerleading team at Sutter High School. I'd have done just about anything to get my folks to hire her as the babysitter any night of the week.

Ronie came running down the stairs. She stopped next to me, bouncing on her toes, and rubbed my head. "Rylee Martin, huh, little man?"

I smacked her hand away. "It's just a suggestion."

Ronie grinned. You wouldn't look at Ronie and see a gymnast. She'd dyed her hair almost black and she had on baggy jeans and one of Dad's t-shirts. But she was actually really good. And when competed she was out to win. She didn't keep any of her trophies in her room. She'd said something about them not being cool once. But Mom kept them all in the garage—and there were a lot of them.

"At least you'll be *safe* with Aunt Rebecca," Ronie said, just quiet enough so I could hear her but my parents wouldn't.

I clenched my back teeth and let out a scream in my head. Mom must have seen something on my face. She put a hand on my shoulder and said, "Oh, c'mon, Jared. She's not so bad."

"Mom, last time she watched me brush my teeth and freaked out when I used more than a pea-sized amount of toothpaste. She thought I'd swallowed some and actually called poison control!"

My dad laughed. "These will be great stories one day. You really should write them down."

My mom kissed my head. "So she's a bit cautious. Remember, she worked for an insurance company for years. She knows how dangerous the world can be."

I knew the story, of course. She used to work as an insurance adjuster and she'd gone to all these crazy accidents and wrote reports on how they could have been avoided. According to my mom, it got to her. She'd apparently developed some kind of post-traumatic stress and started seeing danger everywhere. I felt bad for her, but I didn't understand why I had to put up with her brand of crazy. Especially when there was a perfectly hot babysitter down the street.

"You'll be fine," Mom said. "We'll be back tomorrow evening about this time."

She bent down to hug and kiss Sky, and I thought about not being in the house tomorrow. If I could get out early enough, I might not even have to see Aunt Rebecca the whole day.

"Have fun, you two," Mom said. She hugged and kissed us

both a second time, and then my dad hugged and kissed Sky. He reached out to do the same to me. I held up my hand and shook my head. I was a Revenger—Revengers weren't huggers.

Mom called back as she headed toward the car, "Jared, look after your sister, okay? Your aunt just texted—she's only a few minutes away."

I nodded and muttered, "Not my aunt."

After they drove off, I slumped against the doorway, wondering what I was going to do. Aunt Rebecca's post-traumatic paranoia about safety meant that she was hyper aware of everything. She'd know if I was sneaking around. She'd probably bring helmets and kneepads and force us to wear them just to walk around the house. In fact, if Sky had any money at all, I'd have bet her we'd both be wearing bubble-wrap jackets before the end of the day.

I grabbed the phone off the counter and punched in Marcus's number.

"Hey, it's me," I said.

"Hey, man, I was just working on that new website. I feel way better now that we're out of that heat. When are you coming over? I've got a few ideas about that other thing we're working on."

That other thing? Obviously one of his parents were nearby. "Yeah, about that. I'm not a hundred percent sure I'll be able to get over to your place tonight." I glanced down at Sky who was galloping a plastic pony over the wall beside me.

"Why?" Marcus asked.

I wasn't sure what to say. I knew what would happen if I told him my parents had hired a sitter for me and Sky. I groaned and decided to just do it like I was pulling off a Band-Aid. "My parents just took off, and—"

"Perfect!" Marcus said, not letting me finish. "My parents are going out to dinner tonight too. It'll give us time to lock down this florist thing."

"Marcus, I need you to focus and listen to me. It's going to be tougher to meet up because…" I let the words fade into a sigh.

"Why? Spit it out already."

"My folks hired a babysitter," I blurted. "I have to wait until she gets here and I may have to stay to help look after Sky."

A long pause came over the phone line. Like I'd thought, Marcus started to laugh.

"Thanks, man," I told him. "That makes me feel so much better."

He stopped laughing abruptly. "Wait, is it that the hot babysitter who lives on your block?"

"Do you think I'd be complaining if it was Rylee?" I asked.

"Guess not." He started laughing again. When he had it almost under control he choked out, "That's so funny, man. I haven't had a sitter since I was, like, three or something."

"Yeah, yeah. I know. My parents said she's not here for me. She'll be looking after Sky."

"Riiiight." Marcus gave another laugh. I couldn't blame

him. I would have been laughing at him if he'd been the one stuck with a sitter. "Okay. If we can't get together tonight we should meet up early tomorrow."

"Sounds good," I said. "See you then."

After I hung up I lowered my head to the countertop. Some assassin I was, left with a babysitter.

Sky tugged on my jeans and whispered, "Jared?" She swiped a lock of brown hair out of her eyes and said, "Is Aunt Rebecca really a zombie?"

"Do you even know what a zombie is?" I asked.

She put her hands on her hips. "Of course I do. Dead people who come back to life and eat brains."

I considered going for it and making Sky think Aunt Rebecca was a zombie. But Sky was only six, and I couldn't bring myself to freak her out like that. Maybe that would have been funny if she didn't still believe in the Tooth Fairy or Santa Claus. Instead, I shook my head. "I was kidding, Sky. Aunt Rebecca is not a zombie. She's just a lady who smells like cinnamon."

A sharp knock shook the front door.

One night, I told myself as Sky and I headed to the front door. *I can handle one night.*

When I opened the door, there was Aunt Rebecca, looking slightly disheveled and anxious. A roll of bubble wrap poked out from under one arm and she hefted a duffle bag in the other hand.

Bubble wrap? I'd only been kidding to think of that but it didn't look like she was kidding at all.

READ THE SERIES
BE PART
OF THE MAYHEM!

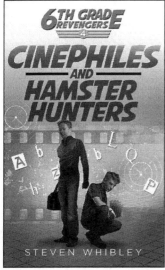

*If you liked this book,
check out these other books
by STEVEN WHIBLEY*

About the Author

Steven Whibley is the author of several middle grade and young adult novels. He lives in British Columbia with his wife and two (soon to be three) young children. If you would like to connect with Steven, please check out his website at www.StevenWhibley.com

Made in the USA
Middletown, DE
04 December 2016